Junie B. Jones Is (almost) a Flower Girl

by Barbara Park

illustrated by Denise Brunkus

A STEPPING STONE BOOK™

Random House New York

To my "bestest" good friend, Sunny Hall.
What would I do without you?

Text copyright © 1999 by Barbara Park
Illustrations copyright © 1999 by Denise Brunkus
All rights reserved under International and Pan-American Copyright
Conventions. Published in the United States by Random House, Inc.,
and simultaneously in Canada by Random House of Canada Limited,
Toronto.

www.randomhouse.com/kids

Library of Congress Cataloging-in-Publication Data
Park, Barbara.
Junie B. Jones is (almost) a flower girl / by Barbara Park ;
illustrated by Denise Brunkus.
  p.   cm. "A Stepping Stone book."
SUMMARY: Six-year-old Junie B. is disappointed to find out that her aunt
has asked someone else to be the flower girl at her wedding.
ISBN 0-375-80038-7 (trade) — ISBN 0-375-90038-1 (lib. bdg.)
[1. Weddings—Fiction.] I. Brunkus, Denise, ill. II. Title.
PZ7.P2197Jtwn   1999   [Fic]—dc21   99-17611

Printed in the United States of America   30 29 28 27 26 25 24 23 22
A STEPPING STONE BOOK and colophon are trademarks of Random House, Inc.

Contents

1/ Ricardo

My name is Junie B. Jones. The B stands for Beatrice. Except I don't like Beatrice. I just like B and that's all.

I am a bachelorette.

A bachelorette is when your boyfriend named Ricardo dumps you at recess. Only I wasn't actually expecting that terrible trouble.

It happened today on the playground.

First I was playing horses with my friends Lucille and Grace.

Then, all of a sudden, my boyfriend

named Ricardo runned right past me.

And he was chasing a new girl named Thelma!

"RICARDO!" I hollered real loud. "HEY! RICARDO! 'ZACTLY WHAT DO YOU THINK YOU ARE DOING, MISTER?"

Then I zoomed right after that guy. And I tackled him on the grass. And we wrestled. And tangled. And rolled all around.

Finally, I sat on his legs. And I smoothed my hair very attractive.

"Hello, Ricardo," I said. "How are you today? I am fine. Only I just saw you chasing new Thelma. And so please knock it off. And I mean it."

Ricardo raised his eyebrows very surprised.

"Why? How come?" he said.

I sucked in my cheeks at that guy.

"*Because*, Ricardo. Because I am your girlfriend. And you are my boyfriend. And boyfriends and girlfriends are only allowed to chase each other. That's how come."

Ricardo kept on looking at me.

I shrugged my shoulders. "Sorry. Those are just the rules," I explained.

Ricardo's face turned very glum.

"But I *like* chasing new Thelma," he said kind of whiny. "It's fun."

I patted his arm very understanding.

"Yes, well, I don't make the rules, Rick. I just enforce them," I said.

After that, I got off his legs. And I sat in the grass next to him.

Ricardo didn't talk for a long time.

Then finally, he stood up. And he shook my hand real nice.

"Junie B., it's been fun being your

boyfriend," he said. "But I think it's time we started chasing other people."

After that, he waved good-bye. And he ran off to chase new Thelma again.

My eyes got big and wide at him.

"NO, RICARDO!" I shouted. "NO, NO, NO! COME BACK! COME BACK!"

But Ricardo kept right on running.

I felt weakish and sickish inside.

I slumped back down in the grass. Only too bad for me. Because just then, the bell rang for the end of recess. And all the children started running to the building.

But not me.

I just kept sitting and sitting in the grass.

My teacher called my name.

Her name is Mrs. She has another name, too. But I just like Mrs. and that's all.

Finally, Mrs. came out to get me.

"Junie B., honey?" she said. "Why aren't you coming in? What's the trouble?"

I looked up real depressed.

"Ricardo," I said real sad. "Ricardo is the trouble."

After that, tears came in my eyes. And my nose started to run very much.

Mrs. closed her eyes.

"Oh no. Not boy problems," she said. "Not *already*."

After that, she gave me a tissue.

And she stood me on my feet.

And she walked with me to Room Nine.

2/ Grinded

Mother had the day off from work.

She met me at my bus stop.

She was pushing my baby brother named Ollie in his carriage.

I ran and hugged her legs.

"Mother! Mother! I am so glad to see you!" I said. "'Cause today was the worstest day of my life. I have been run through the *milk*, I tell you."

Mother raised her eyebrows kind of confused.

"Oh. I think you mean the *mill*, Junie B.," she said. "*Run through the mill* means you've had a hard, grinding day."

I nodded my head.

"Yes, Mother. That's 'zactly what kind of day I had. 'Cause my boyfriend named Ricardo wants to chase other people. And that news grinded me right into the ground."

I reached in my pocket and pulled out my snack cookie.

"Look. See how upset I was, Mother? I couldn't even eat my snack cookie at snack time. 'Cause my stomach felt squeezy and sickish inside."

Mother took my snack cookie out of my hand.

She took a big delicious bite of it.

"Mmm. Thank you, honey," she said.

I stared and stared at that woman. 'Cause she missed the point, apparently.

"No, Mother. You are not supposed to *eat* my snack cookie," I said. "You are supposed to feel sorry for me. Plus also you have to tell me how to get Ricardo back."

Mother bended down and gave me a hug.

"I'm sorry, honey. I know that you're upset about Ricardo. But really and truly, Junie B., you are *way* too young to have a boyfriend."

She stood back up and smiled. "You're just a little girl," she said.

I stamped my foot.

"No, I am *not* little!" I said back. "And anyway, all the girls at school have boyfriends, Mother! My bestest friend Lucille has a boyfriend named Clifton. And my other bestest friend Grace has a boyfriend named Roger. And Charlotte has a boyfriend named Ham. And Rose has a boyfriend named Vincent. And Lynnie has a boyfriend named Crybaby William. And now I am all alone with nobody."

Mother did a sigh.

"I'm sorry, honey. But *all* of those girls are too young to have boyfriends," she said. "Please, Junie B. Do not start this boy stuff so soon. Little girls are supposed to be footloose and fancy-free."

I did a frown.

"What's loose feet got to do with this problem?" I asked.

Mother laughed. "It's just an expression, Junie B.," she said. "*Footloose and fancy-free* means that you can run and play with anyone you want."

She ruffled my hair.

"You don't have to worry about picking out a boyfriend till you're much, much older," she said.

I did a huffy breath at her.

"But I'm already much, much older!" I said. "And besides, I don't want loose feet! I want the same kind of feet everybody else has. I'm not a baby, you know."

I quick runned over to Ollie. And I held up his teensy hand.

"See this, Mother? This is a baby hand. See how teensy it is?"

I held my hand right next to it.

"Now look at *my* hand. See how big it is next to Ollie's? Huh, Mother? Do you?"

After that, I picked up one of Ollie's baby feet.

"And see this teensy foot? My feet are a

bajillion times bigger than these little baby
things."

I stood up straight and tall.

"I am big, I tell you! I am big like a giant
lady, practically!"

Mother did a chuckle.

"Sorry, toots. But I'm afraid you're still too young for a boyfriend," she said.

After that, she gave me another hug.

And she smoothed my hair.

And she ate the rest of my snack cookie.

3/ Being a Grown-up Lady

At dinnertime, I told Daddy about what happened on the playground.

And guess what?

He said the same dumb thing as Mother!

"You're way too young to have a boyfriend, Junie B.," he said. "It's nice to have Ricardo as a friend. But little girls should be footloose and fancy-free."

I covered my ears when I heard that.

"Quit saying that about my feet!" I said.

"I don't *want* loose feet, I tell you! I want grown-up feet just like Mother has!"

Just then, Mother looked at Daddy.

"I think someone is s-l-e-e-p-y," she spelled.

I did a mad breath at her.

"Yeah, only guess what? I'm a grown-up lady. And grown-up ladies know how to spell. And so I am not one bit *slippery*. So there."

Then Mother did a chuckle. Only I don't know why.

After that, she got me down from the table. And she took me in the bathroom. And she filled up the tub for my bath.

She put lots of bubbles in the water.

Also, she gave me bath toys. And a washcloth puppet.

I gave them right back to her.

"These things are for babies," I said. "And I am all grown up."

"Suit yourself," said Mother.

After that, she sat down on the floor. And she watched me sit in the bubbles.

I sat and sat and sat.

"See me, Mother? See how I am just sitting here?" I said. "When grown-up ladies take a bath, we just sit in the water. And we don't splash. And we don't play with baby toys."

I sat and sat some more.

Then finally, I did a big sigh.

'Cause I was bored out of my mind, that's why.

I patted the bubbles a little bit.

"Sometimes grown-up ladies pat the bubbles," I said. "It is not the same as playing."

Mother smiled.

I picked up some bubbles and put them on my arms.

"Bubbles are good for ladies' skin," I said again. "They make us very smoothie."

I put bubbles on my face and chin.

"Sometimes grown-up ladies enjoy

making a bubble beard," I explained very serious.

After that, I covered my whole entire self with bubbles.

"Hey! It is very fluffery in here!" I said real happy.

Mother laughed.

"You look like a bride in a long white veil," she said.

Then, all of a sudden, her whole entire mouth came open.

"Oh my gosh! I almost forgot to tell you the good news, didn't I?" she said. "Your Aunt Flo called today! And she said she's getting *married!*"

Mother clapped her hands together.

"Aunt Flo, Junie B.! Aunt Flo is getting married! Isn't that *exciting?* You're going to go to your very first wedding!"

After that, Mother smiled real big.

And she hummed a pretty bride song.

And she danced with my towel.

And so guess what?

Getting married must be a very big deal.

4/ Flower Girls

The next day at recess, I sang the pretty bride song.

I sang it to my bestest friends named Lucille and that Grace.

"HERE COMES THE BRIDE…
ALL DRESSED AND WIDE…
HER NAME IS CLYDE,
AND SHE READS *TV GUIDE*."

That Grace looked admiring at me.

"Wow. I never even knew that song had words," she said.

"Of course it has words, silly. Every song has words," I said. "All you have to do is make them up."

After that, I skipped all around those two. And I sang the song some more.

"Guess why I'm singing this bride song?" I asked. "Guess, people! Guess! Guess! Guess!"

I couldn't wait for them to guess.

"'CAUSE I'M GOING TO MY FIRST WEDDING EVER! ON ACCOUNT OF MY AUNT FLO IS GETTING MARRIED! THAT'S WHY!"

Lucille clapped her hands real delighted.

"A wedding! A wedding! I *love* weddings, Junie B.! Are you going to be the flower girl? Huh? Are you? Are you?"

I wrinkled my eyebrows.

"The what?" I asked. "The who?"

"The flower girl! The flower girl!" said Lucille. "The flower girl is the very first person to walk down the aisle at the wedding! She gets to carry a flower basket. And she throws beauteous flower petals all over the floor."

"It's really fun, too, Junie B.!" said

Grace. "I was the flower girl at my Aunt Lola's wedding. And I got to wear a long satin dress! And I only tripped two times!"

Lucille fluffed her fluffy hair.

"Yes, well, *I've* been the flower girl in *three* weddings. Grace," she said. "And I've worn *three* long satin dresses. And all of them had matching purses and shoes and hats. Plus one of them had a blue fake bunny fur cape. And I *never* tripped at all. So that makes me the best flower girl, probably."

Grace's face drooped a teeny bit.

"Oh," she said kind of soft.

After that, Lucille asked me a million more questions.

"What kind of flower girl dress are you going to wear, Junie B.? Huh? Is it going to be long or short? What color will it be, do you think? So far I have worn yellow and pink and blue."

She tapped on her chin.

"Hmm. I wonder what kind of flower petals you will carry in your flower basket? Tell your Aunt Flo that I prefer rose petals."

All of a sudden, Lucille did a gasp.

"Junie B.! Junie B.! I just thought of something! Maybe Grace and I can *teach* you! We can teach you how to walk down the aisle and carry the basket! Want us to? Huh? Want us to teach you?"

I jumped up and down.

"Yes!" I said. "Of course I want you to, Lucille!"

After that, Grace cheered up very much. Then all of us did a high five.

And we skipped in a happy circle.

And we practiced being flower girls.

5/ Bo

I skipped home from my bus stop very thrilled. 'Cause I had good news, of course!

My grampa Miller was babysitting baby Ollie. They were playing on the floor together.

I runned and jumped on the couch.

"GRAMPA MILLER! HEY, GRAMPA MILLER! LISTEN TO MY GOOD NEWS! I'M GOING TO BE THE FLOWER GIRL AT AUNT FLO'S WEDDING! AND SO WHAT DO YOU THINK OF THAT, SIR?"

Grampa Miller stopped playing with Ollie.

He did a funny look at me.

"What?" he said. "Are you *sure* about that, toots?"

"Sure I'm sure! Of course I'm sure!" I said. "'Cause me and my friends decided it at school today! And now all I need to do is tell Aunt Flo!"

I zoomed to the kitchen and got my mother's address book.

Then I zoomed right back to my grampa.

"Here, Grampa Miller! Tell me Aunt Flo's phone number. I need to call her right this very minute!"

Grampa Miller scratched his head.

"Gee, I don't know, honey," he said. "This doesn't sound like a good idea to me. What if Aunt Flo has already made arrangements for a flower girl?"

I laughed out loud at that silly man.

"Yeah, only how could she already make arrangements for a flower girl, when she doesn't even know it's me yet?"

Grampa Miller covered his face with his hands. He did a groan back there, I think.

I pulled on his sleeve.

"Come on, Grampa! Look up the number! Please? Please? Please?" I begged.

Finally, Grampa shaked his head no.

"You really need to wait and discuss this with your mother," he said.

I did a huffy breath at that guy.

'Cause Mother would not be home for an hour, probably! And who could wait *that* long?

That's how come I quick hided the address book under my arm. And I tippy-toed down the hall to Mother's room.

Then I closed her door very secret. And I climbed up on her bed.

After that, I opened up the address book to the page with the M's. 'Cause Aunt Flo's last name is Miller! Just like my grampa's!

And what do you know!

I spied it right away!

"F-L-O," I spelled real thrilled. "F-L-O SPELLS FLO!"

And here's another good thing! Aunt Flo's phone number was right next to her name!

"Hey! This project was easy as cake!" I said.

After that, I dialed the number speedy quick.

It ringed and ringed.

"Hello?" said a voice.

I did a gasp.

"HEY! WHAT DO YOU KNOW! I DID IT, AUNT FLO! I CALLED YOU RIGHT ON THE TELEPHONE!"

Aunt Flo's voice sounded curious.

"Junie B.?" she said. "Is that *you?*"

"YES! YES! IT'S ME, AUNT FLO! IT'S JUNIE B. JONES! AND I'VE GOT THE BESTEST SURPRISE YOU EVER HEARD OF!"

Then, all of a sudden, the surprise popped right out of my mouth.

"I'M GOING TO BE THE FLOWER GIRL AT YOUR WEDDING, AUNT FLO! AND SO THIS IS YOUR LUCKY DAY, MADAM!"

I runned all over the bed.

"Wait till you see me, Aunt Flo! I will be the bestest flower girl you ever saw! 'Cause

Lucille already showed me how to throw flower petals! And Grace showed me how not to trip!"

I kept on talking very excited.

"Mother thinks I'm a baby, Aunt Flo. But I'm not! I'm a grown-up lady! Wait till you see me! Just wait till you see me!"

Aunt Flo didn't say any words.

I tapped on the receiver with my fingers.

"Aunt Flo? Aunt Flo? Where did you go?"

Finally, she talked again.

"Uh…yes, well…I'm here, Junie B.," she said. "It's just that your news sort of caught me…off guard."

I bounced on the bed some more.

"Hurray!" I said. "Hurray for off guard, right, Aunt Flo? 'Cause off guard is like a big surprise, right? And so what kind of dress would you like me to wear? I think it should be long…all the way to the floor."

I grinned real big.

"And guess what else? Maybe I will also wear a blue fake bunny fur cape!"

Aunt Flo didn't talk again.

I looked into the phone with my eyeball.

"Hmm. We musta got a bad connector here," I said.

"Junie B., honey," said Aunt Flo. "I'm afraid I have some bad news for you."

Just then, I felt sickish in my stomach. 'Cause bad news is not that good, usually.

My voice got quieter.

"What *kind*, Aunt Flo?" I asked very nervous. "What *kind* of bad news?"

"Oh dear. I don't really know how to tell you this, Junie B. But…well, Joe and I have already chosen a flower girl for the wedding, honey. And, uh, I'm afraid it's not you."

I did a gulp.

"Who are you afraid it *is?*" I asked even quieter.

"It's Bo," said Aunt Flo.

"Bo?"

"Bo is Joe's little sister," said Aunt Flo.

"Joe?"

"Joe is the man I'm marrying," said Aunt Flo. "Joe asked Bo."

"Oh," I whispered.

Just then, my eyes got tears in them.

"I gotta go," I said.

After that, my nose started to run very much.

And I hanged up the phone.

6/ The Alternate

The rest of the day was not that enjoyable.

I got in big trouble.

'Cause Aunt Flo tattletaled to Grampa Miller. And Grampa Miller tattletaled to Daddy. And Daddy tattletaled to Mother.

And Mother made a big issue of it at dinner.

A *big issue* is the grown-up word for Mother keeps yelling and yelling and she won't let the matter drop.

"It was *wrong*, Junie B. Jones," she said.

"It was *wrong* to disobey your grandfather. And it was *wrong* to invite yourself to be in Aunt Flo's wedding."

I sat up a little straighter.

"Flo," I said kind of soft. "F-l-o spells Flo."

Mother sucked in her cheeks.

"Yes…well, we're all thrilled that you're learning to spell. But this isn't about spelling, Junie B. This is about disobeying your grandfather."

I hanged my head way down.

"But I wanted to be a flower girl real bad," I said. "I wanted to wear a long dress and show you I'm a grown-up lady."

Mother did a frown. "I'm sorry, but that's no excuse," she said.

After that, I slumped way far over at the table. Only too bad for me. 'Cause my head got too close to my plate. And my hair got gravy on it.

I stared and stared at my gravy hair.

"Today is not actually going that well," I said to just myself.

Just then, the phone rang.

Mother answered it.

Oh no!

It was Aunt Flo!

And she wanted to talk to *me!*

Mother handed me the phone.

I shook my head real fast.

"No, thank you. I don't actually care to speak to her at this time," I said.

But Mother kept on shoving the phone at me. And so I didn't have a choice.

My insides felt shaky and nervous.

"H…h…hello?"

"Why, hello, yourself!" said Aunt Flo.

Her voice sounded jolly.

"I'm sorry about what happened today, Junie B.," she said. "But I've got some good news for you. How would you like to be the *alternate* flower girl? Do you know what an alternate is?"

I shook my head no.

"An alternate is like a *substitute*, sort of," she said. "Like if Bo gets sick and she can't be in the wedding…*you* will step in and be the flower girl! Do you understand, honey?"

Just then, I felt a little bit happier inside.

"I do, Aunt Flo. I do understand," I said.

"But wait," said Aunt Flo. "I haven't even told you the best part yet! Because even if Bo doesn't get sick, we still want you to sit with the bridesmaids at the reception! How does that sound?"

My eyes got biggish and widish.

"Perfect! It sounds perfect!" I said real squealy.

I jumped down from my chair.

"Hey, Aunt Flo! This means I can still wear a long dress, right? And who knows? Maybe Bo will even give me a couple of flower petals for my very own!"

I kept on getting happier and happier.

"Thank you, Aunt Flo! Thank you for making me the alternate flower girl! 'Cause this day turned out happier than I thought!"

After that, I quick hanged up the phone.

And I zoomed all around the house like a rocket!

Also, I did a cartwheel!

And I standed on my head!

'Cause now Mother will get to see what a grown-up lady I really, really am!

7/ Hope

Mother bought me a beautiful dress for the wedding.

It had golden puffery sleeves. And it came all the way to the floor.

Also, she bought me fancy pantyhose with glimmery shimmers on them. And brand-new shiny gold shoes.

I could not thank that woman enough!

I thanked her the whole time I was in the store.

"Thank you, Mother!" I said. "Thank

you for my beautiful dress! Thank you for my fancy pantyhose! And thank you, thank you for my shiny gold shoes!"

I smiled real big.

"Now all I need is my blue fake bunny fur cape. And I will be all set!"

Mother shook her head.

"Oh no. No way," she said. "We've spent quite enough for one day."

I looked and looked at that woman. 'Cause she has no fashion sense, apparently.

"Yes, but I *have* to have a blue fake bunny fur cape, Mother," I said. "Lucille says a blue fur cape adds elegance to any outfit. Lucille says—"

Mother interrupted my words. Her voice sounded scary in my ear.

"I don't care *what* Lucille says," she grouched. "No…fur…cape."

I quick backed up from her.

"All rightie then," I said kind of nervous.

After that, I helped carry my bags to the car. And I behaved myself all the way home.

Then I runned to my house with all my beautiful things. And I tried my flower girl dress on for Daddy.

And guess what else?

I walked all the way down the hall!

And I didn't even trip!

Daddy gave me a thumbs-up.

"What a perfect flower girl you are!" he said real proud.

"Thank you," I said. "Only I'm not the *real* flower girl. Remember, Daddy? I'm just the alternate."

Just then, my shoulders drooped a teeny bit. And I didn't feel that happy anymore.

'Cause at first you're very, very glad to be the alternate.

And after that…

You're not.

That night after dinner, Mother tucked me in bed real snug.

She kissed me good-night on my head.

"Yeah, only don't turn out my light yet. 'Cause I forgot to do something very important," I said.

After that, I quick got out of bed again. And I looked out my window.

"Star light, star bright. First star I see tonight. I wish I may, I wish I might…have the wish I wish tonight."

I crossed my fingers for luck.

"Dear Star, Please make Bo sick for Aunt Flo's wedding. Love, your friend, Junie B. Jones."

I hopped back in my bed.

Mother's eyes got big and wide at me.

"No, Junie B.! Absolutely not!" she said. "We do *not* wish for people to get sick. You go back to that window. And you change that wish right now."

I raised up my eyebrows at her.

"Yeah, only how can I change it? It already got sent," I explained.

"Fine," said Mother. "Then go back to

the window and wish a nicer wish on top of it."

She snapped her fingers and pointed.

"*Now*, Junie B. I mean it."

I got out of bed real slow.

Then I walked to the window again.

And I looked at my same star.

"Dear Star, Mother says not to make Bo sick. And so maybe you could just give her a case of head lice and that's all. Thank you and good night."

Mother shook her head.

"No, Junie B.," she said. "No, no, no."

I did a mad breath.

"But head lice doesn't even *hurt*, Mother," I said back. "Head lice just takes a little extra shampoo. And that's all."

But Mother kept on shaking her head. And she made me change my wish again.

"Okay, Star, never mind the whole dumb thing. Only now I won't be a flower girl for my whole entire life, probably. And so I hope my mother is happy. Amen."

After that, I got back in my bed. And Mother turned out my light.

After she left, I did a big sigh.

"Shoot. That lice idea was a beaut," I said real soft.

Just then, my stuffed elephant named Philip Johnny Bob tapped on me.

Don't feel bad, he said. *You might still get to be the flower girl.*

"Yeah, only how?" I asked him.

He thought and thought.

Maybe Bo's daddy will be driving her to the wedding. And their car will get stucked at a railroad crossing. And the train will be a million bajillion miles long, he said.

I felt a little perkier at that idea.

"Hey, yeah," I said. "Or else maybe his car might get stucked in something else. Like in some ooey gooey mud. Or in a traffic jam. Or in…or in…"

Or in a giant puddle of Krazy Glue! said

Philip Johnny Bob.

After that, me and him laughed and laughed.

Then I hugged that guy very tight.

'Cause he's always giving me hope.

8 / A Little Tussle

Aunt Flo's wedding took forever to get here. I waited for my whole entire life, practically.

Then, one day at breakfast, Mother told me a happy surprise.

"Well, tomorrow is the big day!" she said.

And so what do you know!

MY VERY FIRST WEDDING WAS ALMOST HERE!!!

That night, I could hardly even sleep.

I got up bright and early in the morning.

Then Mother came in my room. And she decorated my hair with a green velvet ribbon. And she helped me get dressed in my flower girl clothes.

Pretty soon, a lady came to babysit for Ollie.

Then me and Mother and Daddy got in our car. And we rode to the church together.

And guess what? There was a million

bajillion people there already!

I hurried up the steps.

Then I stood on my tippytoes. And I looked all around for Bo.

"Where is she, Mother? Where is Bo? Is she sick, do you think? Did her car get stucked in Krazy Glue? I don't see her anywhere! And so maybe I will be the flower girl after all!"

Mother smoothed my hair very nice.

"Honey, I've already talked to Aunt Flo today," she said. "And Bo is feeling fine. She's probably getting dressed with the bridesmaids."

Mother smiled.

"Let's be happy for her, okay?"

I didn't say anything back. 'Cause what's to be happy about? That's what I would like to know.

After that, all of us went inside. And a man named Usher holded out his arm. And he walked Mother to her church seat.

Me and Daddy followed them down the aisle.

And guess what? I still didn't trip!

Three ladies smiled at me.

I smiled back.

"HELLO, LADIES! SEE HOW GOOD I

AM WALKING DOWN THIS AISLE? TOO BAD I'M NOT THE FLOWER GIRL, RIGHT?"

My voice sounded loud in the church.

I like that kind of loud voice.

After I got to my seat, I smoothed my dress very nice.

And guess who I saw?

I saw my Grandma Helen Miller!

She was sitting right in front of me!

I tapped on her head.

"GRANDMA MILLER! IT'S ME! IT'S YOUR GRANDGIRL, JUNIE B. JONES! LOOK HOW GROWN-UP I AM BEING, HELEN!"

Then Grandma smiled and winked. And she said don't call her Helen.

After that, the organ started to play real loud. And everybody stood up.

Then all of us looked at the back of the church.

And what do you know?

I SAW BO!

She was walking right down the aisle! And she was throwing pink flower petals on the floor!

It looked like fun, I tell you!

My heart got pumpy and poundy inside. 'Cause Bo was coming in my direction!

And so that's how come a great idea popped into my head. And it's called *Hey! Maybe Bo wouldn't mind if I took one or two petals out of her basket and threw them! 'Cause that would be fair of her, I think!*

Bo kept getting closer and closer and closer.

And then, all of a sudden…

SHE WAS RIGHT NEXT TO ME!!

I quick reached for her flower basket!

"NO!" shouted Bo.

"YES!" I shouted back.

Then I tried to take some petals out of the basket. But Bo pulled it away from me. And so that's how come I had to pull it right back again. And then me and her got into a little tussle.

Little tussle is the grown-up word for how come she just won't let go of the darned thing!

Then, all of a sudden, my mother reached over. And she pulled my hands right off of the basket.

Her face was steamy mad.

I did a gulp.

"Hello. How are you today?" I said kind of shaky. "I am fine. Only I just wanted two little petals. But that plan did not work out, apparently. And so now I will just behave myself for the rest of the wedding, I think."

After that, I smoothed my skirt.

And I fluffed my hair.

And I acted like my best grown-up lady.

9/ Loose Feet

After the church, everybody went to the reception.

The reception is a big, giant room where you sit at tables. And you listen to loud music. And you eat food and cake.

And then wait till you hear this! The bridesmaids' table was the longest table in the whole entire place!

I runned right to the end of that hugie thing. And guess what? There was a teensy card with my name printed on it!

"Here! Here! I am sitting here!" I hollered to Mother.

Just then, I saw Aunt Flo.

She was coming over with Bo.

"Uh-oh," I said very nervous.

Then I quick hided behind Mother's skirt.

But Aunt Flo didn't even look mad!

She bended down next to me in her beautiful wedding gown. And she held my hand real nice.

"Junie B., honey? I didn't see what happened in the church. But Bo said you tried to take her basket. Is that true?"

I shook my head very fast.

"No, Aunt Flo. I didn't try to take her whole entire basket. I promise. I just wanted two teensy petals and that's all," I said.

I held up two fingers.

"Just this many, Aunt Flo. Just two. 'Cause Bo got all the rest of the petals. And so two would be fair of her, I think."

Aunt Flo looked at Bo.

"Bo, honey? Did you hear that? Junie B. only wanted two little flower petals."

Bo looked shy at me.

Then, all of a sudden, she reached into

her basket. And she gave me two petals!

I smiled real big.

"Hey! That is a nice gesture of you, Bo!" I said.

After that, Bo smiled back at me. And Aunt Flo put us in our chairs.

Bo asked me how old I am.

I sat up straight and tall.

"I am almost six," I said very proud.

Bo did a sad sigh.

"Poo," she said. "I'm only five. I'm *always* the littlest. Always, always, always."

I patted her arm very understanding.

"Don't worry, little Bo. Someday you will be a grown-up lady, just like me," I said.

Bo did a teeny frown.

"You're not a grown-up lady," she said.

"Yes, I am so a grown-up lady, Bo!" I

said back. "Just ask my mother if you don't believe me. 'Cause I acted grown-up for the whole entire wedding, almost."

Just then, I quick put my napkin in my lap.

"See this, Bo? See how I am putting this napkin in my lap? If I was a baby, I would tuck it in my collar. But grown-up ladies put them in their laps."

I sat up even taller.

"And see how straight and tall I am sitting? This is how grown-up ladies sit," I said. "We never slouch and slump."

After that, I sat very still. And I didn't move a muscle.

"Now look at me, Bo," I said out of the corner of my mouth. "See how still I am sitting? I am not even squirming. On account of grown-up ladies do not get ants in their pants, that's why."

I folded my hands very polite.

"Now I am folding my hands very polite. And I am waiting for my food."

Bo kept on looking at me.

"The end," I said.

After that, I kept sitting there a real long time.

That's how come Bo got tired of looking at me. And she started playing with her spoon.

She clinked it on her water glass.

Also, she clinked it on her plate. And her knife. And her head.

"Grown-up ladies do not clink their spoons," I said.

Bo shrugged her shoulders at me.

After that, she made a puppet out of her napkin. And she made it bite my nose.

"Hey!" I said very surprised.

Then I quick did a frown.

"Grown-up ladies do not play with their napkins," I said.

After that, I did a big sigh. 'Cause my food was taking a million thousand years, that's why.

Finally, my legs started to get stiffish and tightish.

Also, I got an ant in my pant.

And my foot went to sleep.

That is how come I had to hop down from my chair. And I stamped my foot on the floor.

"Sometimes ladies have to stamp their sleeping feet," I explained to Bo. "It is perfectly acceptable to do this."

After that, I shaked my foot all around. But it still did not wake up.

I looked at Bo.

"Okay. Here's the thing. Sometimes ladies have to skip around the table to get their blood pumping," I said.

"Really?" said Bo.

"Yes," I said. "Trust me. I know what I'm doing."

After that, I started to skip around the table. Only too bad for me. 'Cause my new shoes hurt my heels a real lot. Plus also my fancy pantyhose drooped all the way down to my knees.

I walked back to my seat very limping.

I looked at Bo again.

"Sometimes ladies have to go under the table and adjust theirselves," I said.

Bo looked curious at me.

"They do?" she asked.

"Of course they do," I said. "That's how

come they make the tablecloths so long."

After that, I ducked under the tablecloth. And I quick took off my shoes. Plus also I took off my pantyhose.

"Ahh. Better," I said.

Then I climbed back onto my chair

again. And I wiggled my piggy toes all around in the air.

"What a relief," I said. "Loose feet."

All of a sudden, my eyes got big and wide! And I did a gasp!

'Cause that reminded me of what Mother and Daddy told me!

"BO! HEY, BO!" I said real thrilled. "LOOSE FEET! GET IT? I HAVE LOOSE FEET!"

"Huh? What?" said Bo.

And so that's how come I told her all about my boyfriend named Ricardo. And how he wanted to chase other people. And how Mother and Daddy said I should have loose feet!

"Get it, Bo? Get it?" I asked. "Mother and Daddy were right! Loose feet *are* funner than grown-up feet!"

After that, I quick got on my knees. And I clinked my water glass with my spoon. Also, I clinked my plate and my fork and my head.

"Sometimes it's fun to be little! Right, Bo? Right? Right?" I said.

Me and Bo clinked spoons.

"Right!" she said real giggly.

After that, I made a puppet out of my napkin. And I made it bite Bo's nose.

And that is not even the best part!

'Cause after lunch, me and Bo skipped around the whole entire room in bare feet! And we throwed flower petals on people's heads! And no one even got mad. 'Cause when you're little, you can get away with those kind of shenanigans!

It was the funnest time I ever had.

And guess what else?

After the reception, me and Bo hugged each other good-bye. And she said she will call me sometime! And I said I will write her a letter!

"Only first I have to learn to spell more words," I said.

Bo shrugged her shoulders.

"That's okay. First I have to learn to read," she said.

After that, both of our daddies picked us up. And they carried us out to the parking lot.

"Hey! Look how high up I am, Bo!" I hollered to her. "I am as tall as a grown-up lady, almost! Only grown-up ladies don't even get carried! And so too bad for them! Right, Bo? Right?"

"Right!" hollered Bo.

After that, we waved good-bye at each other.

First I waved my hand.

Then I waved my whole entire arm.

Plus also I waved all of my ten piggy toes.

I laughed real happy.

"See, Daddy? See? I've got loose feet just like you said!"

Then Daddy laughed, too.

And we sang the pretty bride song all the way to the car.